just
like
brothers

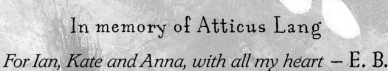

In memory of Atticus Lang

For Ian, Kate and Anna, with all my heart — E. B.

For everyone who is brave enough to explore the unknown — A. B.

Barefoot Books
2067 Massachusetts Ave
Cambridge, MA 02140

Barefoot Books
29/30 Fitzroy Square
London, W1T 6LQ

First published in the United States of America by Barefoot Books, Inc
and in Great Britain by Barefoot Books, Ltd in 2018

Graphic design by Sarah Soldano, Barefoot Books
Art directed by Kate DePalma, Barefoot Books
Reproduction by Bright Arts, Hong Kong
Printed in China on 100% acid-free paper
This book was typeset in Aunt Mildred and LyntonBQ
The illustrations were prepared in acrylics

Hardback ISBN: 978-1-78285-345-9
Paperback ISBN: 978-1-78285-346-6

British Cataloguing-in-Publication Data:
a catalogue record for this book is
available from the British Library

Library of Congress Cataloging-in-Publication Data
is available upon request

1 3 5 7 9 8 6 4 2

just like brothers

written by **Elizabeth Baguley**

illustrated by **Aurélie Blanz**

Barefoot Books
Step inside a story

Not far away, there is a wood
that is tree-thick and thorn-twisty.

And near the wood live a mother
and her brown-eyed child.

The mother says,
"Beware, beware, my brown-eyed child.
Never wander in the woods
where wolves howl.
For you are small and sweet as honey
and the wolves are wild.
They are long-snout and sharp-tooth;
they are rough-fur and claw-paw."

But the brown-eyed child is
moon-mind and shut-ear
and he doesn't listen to his mother.

Instead he chases rabbits.

In the thick of the forest
the forked paths are criss-crossed.

Among branches and brambles
he's suddenly lost.

In the woods
   live a she-wolf and her grey-furred cub.

And the she-wolf says,
   "Beware, beware, my grey-furred cub.
   Never wander in the woods where men prowl.
   For you are small and sweet as acorns
      and the men are mean.
   They are heavy-foot and spy-eye;
      they are rough-hand
         and jab-stick.

But the grey-furred cub is
wag-tail and scamper-paw
and he doesn't listen to his mother.

Instead he chases rabbits.

In the thick of the forest
the forked paths
are criss-crossed.

Among branches and brambles
he's suddenly lost.

Listen!
    A padding of claw-paws!
    The child's eyes open like moons.
    Wolf coming!

Listen!
   A crackling of twist-twigs!
The cub's ears stiffen –
   Man coming!

The wolf mustn't hear me,
thinks the child.

The man mustn't see me,
thinks the cub.

Beware! Beware!
The forest holds its breath.

They freeze
and stare.

"Wild wolf? Where are your
long snout and sharp teeth?"
says the child to the cub.

"Mean man? Where are your
rough hands and jab-stick?"
says the cub to the child.

Then the child's hand is gentle-reach.
"You are soft-fur!" he says.

The cub's snout is shy-sniff.
"And you are kind-touch!" he says.

And soon they're chasing rabbits,
playing hide-find and tumble-ball,
all wide-smile and wag-tail.

But then through the thorn-wood
sneaks a shivering of shadows.
And then through the wild-wood
streaks a whip-wind of leaf-lash.

And the grey cub and
the man child are . . .

. . . gone.

"Where are you, my child?"
cries a mother who wonders.
"Are you taken by wolf-beast?"

"Where are you, my cub?"
howls a mother who wanders.
"Are you stolen by man-brute?"

But their children lie together
hidden from the
whirling weather,
in a bed with leaves like feathers,

safe and sound.

"We must learn to trust each other,"
says the she-wolf to the mother.
"For these two are just like brothers . . .

. . . lost and found."

Barefoot Books
Step inside a story

At Barefoot Books, we celebrate art and story that opens the hearts
and minds of children from all walks of life, focusing on themes that
encourage independence of spirit, enthusiasm for learning and respect
for the world's diversity. The welfare of our children is dependent on
the welfare of the planet, so we source paper from sustainably managed
forests and constantly strive to reduce our environmental impact.
Playful, beautiful and created to last a lifetime, our products combine
the best of the present with the best of the past to educate our
children as the caretakers of tomorrow.

www.barefootbooks.com

Elizabeth Baguley grew up in
Nottinghamshire in the East Midlands of
England, and her earliest memories are of listening
to stories on her mother's knee. Today she is an author,
educator and proud mother to two grown daughters.
www.elizabethbaguley.com

Aurélie Blanz has enjoyed drawing and painting
since she was a child growing up in Germany. She
was especially excited to illustrate *Just Like Brothers*,
because she hopes it will help young readers overcome
a fear of the unknown. Today Aurélie lives in Paris
with her husband and three children.
www.aurelieblanz.com